ISBN 978-0-06-221861-2 (trade bdg.)

The artist used mixed media, hand lettering, and photoshop to create the digital illustrations for this book.

Typography by Martha Rago

14 15 16 17 18   SCP   10 9 8 7 6 5 4 3 2 1

❖

First Edition

Ryan O'Rourke

BELLA
LOST AND FOUND

HARPER
An Imprint of HarperCollinsPublishers

*B*ella came from a long line of great sea cats.

Bella loved to look out the window and imagine having adventures on the high seas like her grandfather, her great-grandfather, and her great-great-grandfather. But she was an indoor cat who lived inside a lighthouse. She never went outside, until one day . . .

Bella slipped through an open door and stepped
outside for the first time.

The salty sea air tickled her whiskers as she
followed a butterfly down to the water's edge.

Then she hopped aboard a tiny
sailboat just her size.

She pretended she was a fierce pirate like her
great-great-grandfather.

A gust of wind came up, and Bella and her boat were pushed out onto the ocean!

WHOO

The waves became choppy and rough. Bella was scared, but she did her best to cling to the boat as it was tossed about.

A great whale surfaced right under Bella's boat. The whale's spray catapulted Bella and her boat high into the air!

With a *THUD!* Bella and her boat came crashing down on the whale's back.

Bella apologized to the great whale.

"I am really just an indoor cat," she explained. "And I have lost my way home."

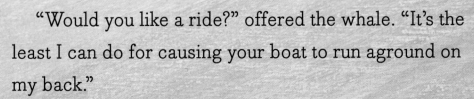

"Would you like a ride?" offered the whale. "It's the least I can do for causing your boat to run aground on my back."

Perhaps this will help me get home, Bella thought as she accepted the whale's kind offer.

Bella and the whale floated through the ocean until they came to a big orange buoy.

"This is as far as I can go," the whale said. "But if you swim all the way down to the ocean floor, you will find my friend Arthur. He knows the ocean better than anyone. He'll be able to help you get home."

So Bella hopped onto the buoy and waved good-bye to the whale.

GooD-Bye!!!!

The little kitty counted to ten, held her breath, then splashed into the sparkling ocean. She pretended she was a deep-sea diver. Although Bella had never liked baths, she had no trouble swimming.

Down and down and down she swam—down until she came upon a giant octopus.

"Are you Arthur?" she asked.

"Indeed I am," replied the octopus.

Bella explained how she had gotten lost and met the whale, who thought Arthur could get her to the shore and on her way home.

Arthur agreed to help, and he stretched out one of his tentacles for the little cat to hold as they made their way to dry land.

When they finally reached the shore, Bella thanked
Arthur for being such a good guide.

"The pleasure was all mine," Arthur replied.

The octopus wished Bella luck, then waved good-bye
with all eight arms.

Bella looked around but could not see the lighthouse. She was still lost.

Far in the distance she saw what looked like cats running through the tall grass.

Bella ran toward the tails hoping to find someone who could help her get back home.

When Bella reached the tall grass, she saw that there weren't any cats there at all.

"Where are all the cats?" she asked some crabs scuttling in the sand.

"Those aren't real cats," a crab replied. "Those are just *cattails*."

"Then who will help me find my way back home to the lighthouse?" Bella cried.

"Well, we can't see over the grass," the crab answered. "But why don't you ask the seagulls? They see everything!"

So Bella made her way through the tall grass to find the seagulls. She could hear them squawking in the distance.

As Bella walked, the sound of the seagulls got louder and louder.

She had to shout to get their attention.

"Excuse me!" she yelled. "Do you know the way to the lighthouse?"

All the seagulls turned to look at the little cat at the water's edge.

"Yes! Yes! We'll show you! Follow us!" they squawked.

The seagulls suddenly took off into the air, leaving poor Bella behind.

"Wait!" Bella shouted, but the seagulls had already flown too far and too high to hear her.

Bella soon found herself alone. It was getting dark.
She missed her friend and wished she had never left
the lighthouse in the first place. The little cat almost
gave up hope, but then she saw a light glowing in
the distance.

BELLA!!!

As Bella started to walk toward it, she thought she could hear someone calling her name. Bella ran and ran and ran, until . . .

aaa!!!!

She could hear her name being called
loud and clear! Bella could see the lighthouse
shining brightly in the night sky.

Suddenly Bella saw her friend waiting for her
in the doorway of the lighthouse.

Bella was greeted with hugs and kisses. She purred
as she nuzzled into his warm embrace. Bella was happy
to be home.

In the days following her adventure, Bella would return to the window, watching the boats chug through the harbor. The little cat felt lucky that she had sailed on the high seas and had still managed to find her way safely home.